Sister Sweet Ella

written and illustrated by
ROSEKRANS HOFFMAN

William Morrow and Company
New York 1982

Printed in the United States of America.
1 2 3 4 5 6 7 8 9 10

Library of Congress Cataloging in Publication Data

Hoffman, Rosekrans.
   Sister Sweet Ella.

   (Morrow junior books)
   Summary: Jealous of his new baby sister, Wadsworth decides to change her into a cat and find another home for her.
   [1. Brothers and sisters—Fiction. 2. Cats—Fiction. 3. Magic—Fiction] I. Title. II. Series.
PZ7.H6758Si   [E]   81-11200
ISBN 0-688-00865-8 AACR2
ISBN 0-688-00866-6 (lib. bdg.)

For Jessmyn,
Jim's great-granddaughter

adsworth wondered why Mama *had* to show Sweet Ella to everyone. The grocer smiled and stuffed beets in her fists. A perfect stranger bent over and gave her lollypops in baskets of jelly beans. And Mrs. Frittle's dogs walked on hind legs just to get a good look at Mama's baby.

"Oh, look, Wadsworth," cried Mama. "Your sister has a new tooth!"

But Wadsworth squeezed his eyes shut until finally Sweet Ella closed her mouth and went to sleep. "Everything was just fine around here until Sweet Ella was born," grumbled Wadsworth.

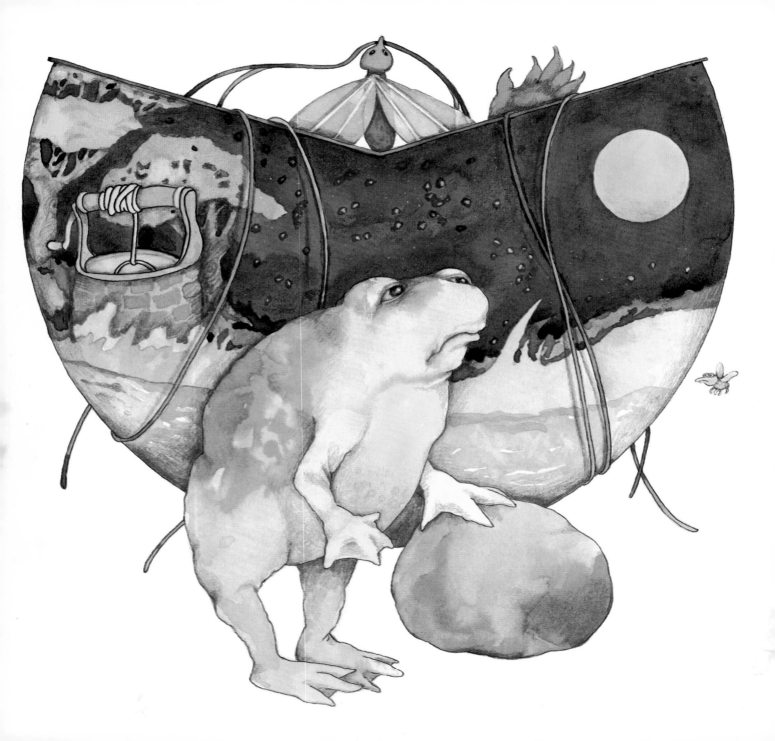

Unable to stand the sight of her another minute, he marched to his room and slammed the door. I'll show old Sweet Ella, thought Wadsworth. I'll turn her into a cat! Mama hates cats!

Wadsworth wiggled his fingers toward his sister's room and chanted in a magical tone of voice:

"Toad in well, Sweet Ella tell,
   to scratch her claw, on midnight stone."

He danced fiercely, shaking his body and rolling his eyes until they hurt. Panting and swaying, he lurched across the room. In one last burst he cried out the window:

"Come Kitty, Kitty-kit,
Come Kitty-kit."

Now Wadsworth waited for the magic to work. He sat down and closed his eyes the way he did when he blew out his birthday candles.

uddenly he felt a rough tongue on his cheek. There, next to his face, was a long, motley-colored cat. The cat looked at him and licked again. He turned his head. "Smelly Ella," he said, holding his nose. "Anyone would think you just came in off the street."

Wadsworth heard Mama's quick steps in the hall. They came closer to his door. Wadsworth had to hide the cat fast. So he pushed her behind him and tried to hold her. "Oh, Wads," cried Mama anxiously, "our little baby dumpling is missing!"

Ugh, thought Wadsworth. And then he felt the cat squirming to get free. Wadsworth hoped Mama wouldn't see. But Mama saw all right. She blinked and shook a shakey finger. "What's that cat doing here?" she screamed. "Get it out of here!" Then she ran from the room, still looking for Sweet Ella.

Wadsworth knew Mama meant what she said. My, he would be glad when this crisis was all over, and he and Mama could settle down and be happy together. Wadsworth lugged his now-hairy sister out of the house. Happiness was so near that Wadsworth could be generous. "I'll find you a good home, Sweet Ella," he said. "Plenty of people will be glad to take *my* sister."

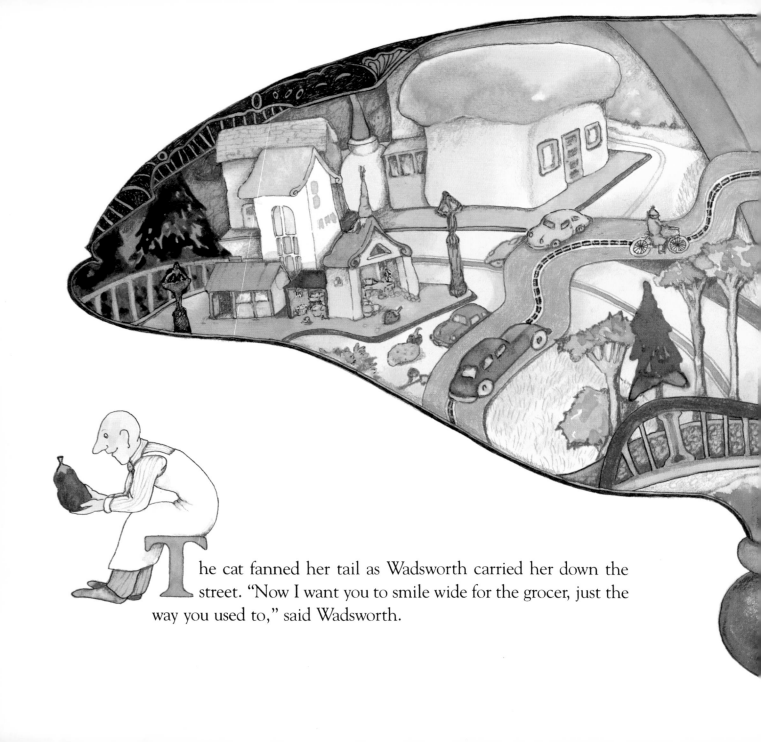

The cat fanned her tail as Wadsworth carried her down the street. "Now I want you to smile wide for the grocer, just the way you used to," said Wadsworth.

They walked into the market and found the grocer behind the beets. Wadsworth stuck Sister Sweet Ella up close to the grocer's face the way Mama did. "I have a good mouser for you, Mr. Grocer," said Wadsworth.

He expected the grocer to stuff beets into the cat's paws and take her to his heart. But before either of them saw what was happening, the cat had clawed the grocer's chin. Wadsworth could see that the grocer did not want Sister Sweet Ella, for he turned abruptly and went grumbling and growling back to his melons and string beans.

Wadsworth and the cat left the market. He was baffled. He wondered how long he would need to get rid of Sister Sweet Ella and if Mama was still looking for the little dumpling. He stopped to smooth the cat's hair and make her presentable. The perfect stranger stopped to watch.

"If you owned this cat, then you would always have a friend," said Wadsworth to the perfect stranger.

"I don't need a friend that badly!" said the perfect stranger. And she walked away without offering so much as a jelly bean.

Wadsworth began to worry. He could not go home and leave his sister on the street. He sat down and held her awhile. How green her eyes were. And he had never noticed. But he was sure Mama had.

Wadsworth and the cat walked to Mrs. Frittle's house, the last chance for a home. "I know Mrs. Frittle would love to take you in, Sister Sweet Ella," said Wadsworth to himself and the cat.

When they arrived, Mrs. Frittle welcomed Wadsworth and the old cat into the living room. She offered Wadsworth and the cat one seat while she and the dogs took the other.

"What an unusual motley-colored cat!" said Mrs. Frittle.

"Oh, this cat comes from fine stock, Mrs. Frittle. I personally know her mother and brother," answered Wadsworth.

"Then she must be your treasure," said Mrs. Frittle.

Suddenly the dogs beside her could contain themselves no longer. They jumped to the floor and ran over to the cat. The cat hissed, the dogs barked, and the chase was on.

Mrs. Frittle went pale as she surveyed the scene. "You'll have to take your cat out of here," she told Wadsworth, "before these animals wreck my house."

Wadsworth's heart sank. He would have to give up. As soon as he could grab the cat, he dashed out of Mrs. Frittle's house.

"Say hello to your mama and Sister Sweet Ella," cried Mrs. Frittle between dog barks.

Poor Wadsworth did the only thing he could do. He carried the cat home in hopes of hiding her under the bed until he could find courage to tell Mama the truth. What a relief it would be to tell Mama how his magic had turned Sweet Ella into a cat.

Wadsworth and the cat sneaked in the front door and tiptoed to his room. He pushed the cat under the bed and listened for Mama, but the house was quiet.

Wadsworth threw himself on the bed and let his hand fall to the floor where the cat was. How cruel magic is, he thought, while the cat pounced at his wiggling fingers.

Just then Mama knocked on his door and entered. *Old Sister Sweet Ella was in her arms!*

"She learned to crawl, and I found her under the table with the long cloth," said Mama, laughing.

Wadsworth could not believe his eyes. Two Sister Sweet Ellas! My magic is out of hand, he thought. First the cat! Now the baby! Of course, Wadsworth *had* wiggled his fingers playing with the cat under the bed, but he hadn't said the magic words. Still, when he looked, the cat was gone.

Sister Sweet Ella was here again, and the motley-colored cat had disappeared. Wadsworth was sorely puzzled, but he wasn't unhappy. Maybe, just maybe, Sweet Ella would be better than a smelly old cat. Maybe magic wasn't always so cruel. Anyway, Wadsworth knew for sure he would think twice before he ever tried any again.

About the Author-Illustrator

Rosekrans Hoffman was educated in her home state of Nebraska. After graduation from college, she assumed a variety of art-related jobs. A professional illustrator since 1973, she has a number of children's books to her credit, including her own *Anna Banana*.

Ms. Hoffman lives with her husband in West Haven, Connecticut.